SAMBO AND SUSAN

JIM THE HUNTSMAN

THE STORY OF A DISOBEDIENT SALMON

Katharine, aged 10 years old,
with her favourite dog and the hounds

FOREWORD
By the Duke of Atholl

The following pages were written and illustrated by my 12-year-old goddaughter Katharine Harrison Wallace without any extraneous aid—

In the hope that they may give as much pleasure to others as they have to her immediate friends it has been decided to publish them as a booklet for old and young — Her godfather hopes that as her age increases she may be able to live up to the high standard of morals which she has so ably championed in these pages —

Atholl

To Mummy,
With love from
Katharine

—

SAMBO AND SUSAN

and other
tales.

Written and illustrated
by

Katharine . Harrison - Wallace .
Aged 12 years.

Published by Collins . 48, Pall Mall, S.W.

CONTENTS

The Adventures of Susan and Sambo.

Once upon a time there was a pony called Sambo, who loved a mare called Susan. She was very beautiful, and always kept her mane in the latest fashion.

Sambo and Susan were engaged to be married, when an awful thing happened, which I will tell you about

SAMBO.

SUSAN.

One day Susan and Sambo were out
for a walk, when a beautiful white
thorough-bred horse came galloping
up. He was very handsome, with a
silver mane.

A BEAUTIFUL WHITE HORSE
CAME GALLOPING UP.

As soon as Susan saw the white horse, she fell in love with him... So she left poor Sambo, and went off with the white horse who was called Oscar.

U ~ ∪ U

SUSAN LEFT POOR SAMBO.

A week later found Sambo still cryin'
he had grown very thin, because he had
had nothing to eat since Susan and
Oscar had gone off.

It was twelve o'clock and Sambo
went for a walk on Exmoor. He went
along the path which he and Susan
had often walked along together. Wher
ever Sambo passed a familiar place,
the tears rolled down his cheeks.

WHEN EVER HE PASSED A FAMILIER PLACE,
TEARS ROLLED DOWN HIS CHEEKS

After a few hours Sambo decided
to go home, he was just wading
through a stream when he
heard a cry of distress from the
valley.
     "HELP! HELP! I am stuck in a bog!"

Sambo recognized the voice to
be that of Susan, so he galloped
down the hillside to save her.
She was gradually sinking, and
Sambo feared he would be too late

At last he got there to find that
Susan had nearly disapeared, only
her head remained above the surface
She was very frightened, and past
all hope. So before Sambo started to
try to get her out, he gave her a loving kiss.

HE GAVE HER A <u>LOVING</u>
KISS.

After a few seconds he thought of
a good plan to save her. He made
her take his tail in her teeth,
and hold on, while he pulled
her out. You will see if this
plan suceeded on the next page! —

HE THOUGHT OF A GOOD PLAN.

At last he got her out of the bog.
She was covered in slimy mud from
head to foot, and still very frightened.
When she grew calmer she told Sambo
how she had got in the bog.

AT LAST HE GOT HER OUT.

She said that Oscar had got tired
of her, so he had pushed her into the
bog to get rid of her!

When she thought of her narrow escape
and how false she had been to poor
Sambo, she burst into tears, and asked
his forgiveness, (which he gave willingly!)

SAMBO FORGAVE HER.

THEY WERE MARRIED.

THE   END

JOCK.
(JIM'S HORSE.)

JIM

the Huntsman.

THE FOX.

CHORISTER
(JIM'S FAVOURITE HOUND.)

It was a hot morning in September, and all the little fox cubs were having a nap in the sunshine. Everything was quiet except for the birds, when suddenly a far-away note of a hunting horn reached their ears.

It was very warm.

Mr Fox pricked up his ears when he heard the hunting-horn, and ordered Mrs Fox and all the cubs to go back into their earth. When they were all in the earth, Mr Fox set off to find if the hounds were near.

He ordered them to go back to their earth.

To Mᵃ Fox's dismay the hounds were very close, so he thought he would slip back to his Earth before they got any closer. But luck was not in his way, because as he crossed a ride, Jim saw him, and shouted "Tally Ho!"

JIM SAW HIM.

Mr Fox was terrified, he knew he mustn't go home, as the hounds would follow him there, and probably kill his wife and cubs. So he set off in another direction, with the hounds and Jim close behind him

Three hours later found Mᴿ Fox still running, he had grown very tired, and he thought that the hounds must kill him soon. He was just struggling across a ploughed field, when he saw a big wood on his right, beside it was a large notice saying:—

There was a notice.

" This is M^{RS} Lawson's wood. "

"Anybody poaching will be fined, "
"as it is an Animal Sanctuary. "
". <u>All</u> hounds and hunting dogs
"will be S H<u>O</u>T if they are "
"found in here."

"By Order. M^{RS} Lawson."

MR Fox was pleased! Here was his
only chance of escape, so he slipped into
the wood.

He slipped into the wood.

In a few minutes time, Jim rode up, he had got in front of hounds. When he read the sign board his face paled and he blew on his horn to stop his hounds. After about ten minutes, with the help of the whip, he managed it. He then took the hounds home as it was late

He blew on his horn.

When the hounds had gone home, M^r
Fox went back to his family and
told them to pack up and come to
Lawson Wood, where he had rented
an earth. It was a very nice one,
so they lived there for many years.

The End

The Foxes Earth.

THE STORY OF

A

DISOBEDIENT SALMON.

Johnnie was a salmon who lived in the River Wye. He was a very naughty salmon as he was so disobedient. His great grandfather was always telling him to be more carefull about being caught by a fisherman, but Johnnie only laughed at him!

JOHNNIE LAUGHED AT HIM.

One day Johnnie's great grand father said to him "You must not go to the Tumbling Pool, as there are fishermen there fishing with large golden sprats." Johnnie said he wouldn't, but that night he had such a lovely dream about golden sprats, that he made up his mind that he would go and eat one the next day,

HE DREAMT ABOUT THE GOLDEN SPRATS.

The next day, Johnnie went down to the Tumbling Pool. He saw a beautiful golden sprat, but he did not see that a line was attatched to it, and that there were some hooks on it. When he had eaten it, he suddenly felt a tug, he was hooked!

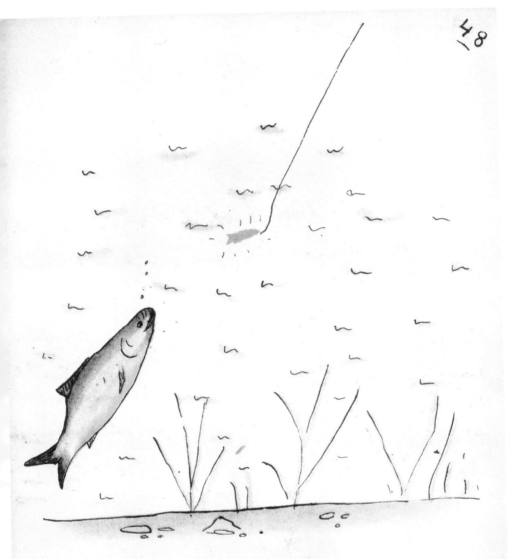

HE SAW A SPRAT.

The boy who had hooked Johnnie was very excited, as he had never hooked a salmon before.

Johnnie was excited, only in a different way. That horrid hook was hurting his throat so. How he wished he had listened to his great grand father's advice!

To get rid of the cruel hooks,
Johnnie jumped out of the water,

raced down to the bottom of
the river,

and rubbed the line
against a large stone.

At last the line broke! Johnnie was proud of himself, although the hook in his mouth still hurt a bit. So he rushed off to his great grand father, to tell him all about it.

THE LINE BROKE

In a few days the hook came out of his mouth, but instead of saying he was sorry he was so disobedient; he was more rude and disobedient than ever.

The next week he was hooked again, and this time he did not escape, but was caught and made into salmon mayonaise, which served him right!

THE END.

HE WAS CAUGHT,

AND MADE INTO SALMON MAYONAISE.

Sambo and Susan and other tales was originally published in 1938 and the first edition, complete with its foreword by Katharine's godfather the Duke of Atholl, developed a cult following and first edition copies are now collector's items commanding a price that the 12 year old Katharine would not have believed possible. The charming stories viewed by many at the time of publication as morality tales, universally appeal to both child and adult alike.

Katharine was extraordinarily clever and sharp witted, as can, I think, be seen from the illustrations and stories she wrote in this book. They are here for you to enjoy – spelling mistakes intact.

My sister, April Strang Steel, and I are delighted to give Sambo and Susan and other tales a new lease of life. Our intention is that proceeds from the sale of this book will go to The Hunt Staff Benefit Society – a registered Friendly Society overseen by its patron, the Prince of Wales, and benefitting the staff without whom fox hunting could not exist. As an enthusiastic member of the hunting field, hunting up to three days a week in adulthood, our mother Katharine would have approved.

Colin Studd

Unfortunately, in this politically correct time the title of the book could offend. We had the option of changing the title, but did not for historical reasons as it goes without saying that we have no wish to upset or defame anyone.

The name "Sambo" is a diminutive of Samuel and its origin is Hebrew meaning "asked by God".

CPSIA information can be obtained
at www.ICGtesting.com
Printed in the USA
LVIC041503051112
3148LVUK00001B